Blue in the Seed

Blue in the Seed

by Kim Yong Ik

Illustrated by Artur Marokvia

LITTLE, BROWN AND COMPANY

Boston   Toronto

Published simultaneously in Canada
by Little, Brown & Company (Canada) Limited

PRINTED IN THE UNITED STATES OF AMERICA

Blue in the Seed

❁ *1* ❁

ALONG the hill road tall grass and slender broom
sedge were waving, and pale heads of dandelions burst
and flew away in strands finer than threads of silk.
The bells on the ox's neck tinkled in time with the
distant clangs of the bell buoys that the wind brought
from the harbor.

"Bok," Omanee said with spirit in her voice, "in
this new place where we are going, it may be that
some will call you 'Fish Eye.' They would like to
see you cry. You may hit them back, but don't cry in
front of them."

"I know all that," replied Chun Bok. "I am pretty
good at hitting."

He turned his gaze to the oxcart piled high with

bundles, wondering if he should have spoken. He did not want his mother to know that he had already been called "Fish Eye" many times. He would return home bruised after a fight whenever his playmates called him that, but he never told his mother why he had fought. He would like to know whether she minded having blue eyes different from other people's dark eyes, but he did not venture to ask.

Omanee went on: "If you study hard in the new school on the mainland and become important, everyone can see that your blue eyes are lucky."

"It is strange about eyes." Chun Bok's broad forehead wrinkled. "Everyone has dark eyes, but I have blue eyes, you have blue eyes and your mother had blue eyes. Did your mother's mother have blue eyes?"

"I do not know," answered Omanee. "It is blue in the seed and that is all I know."

The island markets stretched out along the road that led to the dock, and Omanee and Chun Bok were soon in the bustling noise. Men selling shellfish and edible seaweed were haggling loudest with boat owners who would buy them to take to the mainland for resale. On market days Chun Bok's father would be among those men to sell the seaweeds his mother had fetched under water. Chun

Bok often came with him. Near the dock a barker was spieling for a dog-and-monkey circus and a magician:

> *Two coins for two eyes.*
> *One coin for one eye.*
> *No coin for no eye.*
>
> *Far seats for far eyes.*
> *Near seats for near eyes.*
> *Middle seats for good eyes.*

Chun Bok's father would ask him teasingly how many smiling good eyes he had. When Chun Bok broke into a smile and held out two fingers, his father would give him two coins for him to sit in the middle behind the nearsighted.

Omanee took Chun Bok's hand, saying, "There is no time for a faraway look. The machine boat will leave us if we do not hurry."

At the dock the farmer Pak rose from the crouching position in which he had been sipping wine. He said to the wine vendor, "There, wipe your eyes and look at my friend's ox." Stepping forward, he stroked caressingly the ox's shoulder. He would take the animal's place to pull the borrowed cart back home.

The farmer Pak spoke apologetically. "It is too early for wine, but I thought a bowl of wine might help me to part from this ox." The ox had been hired out to the Pak farm after Chun Bok's father's death. Omanee wanted to sell the ox to Pak, because the ox, she said, reminded her too much of her dead husband, but Chun Bok had begged, cried and insisted that they keep the ox.

Soon boatmen in tight Western trousers talking and laughing came over from the floating dock to help Pak and Omanee unload the cart. Chun Bok unhitched the ox from the cart to lead him aboard. He saw an old woman running toward them, shouting, "How many thousand times did I tell you not to leave the island?"

"Grandmother is coming!" exclaimed Chun Bok, excited because he knew Omanee did not wish to see the quarrelsome old woman.

She was thin and bony, her gray hair streaming back from her pinched face. There was a wheeze in her voice. "When the hill paths are white with people, do you think you could keep me from knowing that you are going?"

She seized Chun Bok's arm and spoke in lower tones. "You are to stay with me while your mother

6

goes away." Then her tone swiftly changed back to anger as she turned on Omanee. "You can't take my only son's only son with you, unfaithful woman. With your fish eyes you are going to search for a new husband."

"I am not looking for any man," responded Omanee promptly. "I do not want to raise my boy on an island where he and his mother are called 'Fish Eye.'" Omanee's lips quivered even after she bit them tight.

"And the ox!" the old woman shouted. "If you take my grandson, you should at least leave us the fine ox that belonged to my son."

As she rushed forward to seize the halter of the animal, the farmer Pak quickly grabbed the woman and held her from behind. The old woman wailed, swinging her arms aimlessly.

Omanee, carrying the bundle of quilt on her head, hurried over the crosspieces of the pier. Chun Bok followed, dragging his ox by the halter.

The machine boat began to clatter, and puffs of smoke rose from the stack. Safely aboard, Chun Bok watched the shifting crowd on the dock and the cattle on the island mountain recede in the distance. Omanee sank down on the sack of dry seaweed beside the ox and, smoothing her ruffled hair, sighed easily. "Bok." She turned, her blue eyes sparkling under dark brows, the long cords of her topcoat fluttering in the briny wind. "Do not linger here to look back on the island we have left. Go to the bow to watch for the headland."

❀ *2* ❀

THE journey ended at a seaside village, two mountains across from the big harbor town, Choong Moo. From the backyard of the new house Chun Bok could gaze on a long gray building against the green side of the hill. It was of wood with a tile roof, and the sun on its glass windows sent thousands of silken rays toward the village. This was the school. Along with the good grazing grass and abundant stream water, it had been the reason for Omanee's choice of this mainland village.

The house faced southward to the sea. It consisted of a narrow porch and one small room with a lean-to kitchen toward a brook. The walls were of stones and mud; the roof was the usual straw thatch. Omanee had selected a little house not only because of the smaller cost but because the annual roofing would require less straw.

The ox shed was in front of the house. Between the house and shed was a neglected patch of ground with pepper plants and pumpkin vines. Before cleaning the shed, Chun Bok put up sticks for the vines so they could eventually reach the roof. He and his mother had begun to plan a garden.

The early morning after they arrived was bright with clean clouds floating high above the mountains. Under the sea wind the barley moved in great green waves. Omanee announced to Chun Bok, "Today you are going with me to school."

"Oma, I don't like going to school," he whined.

"Don't you want to learn many things like other boys?"

"Yes," Chun Bok admitted, "I do, but I don't want to go to school."

Omanee put on her full white skirt and yellow bodice of unbleached grass linen. She parted her hair neatly and used ashes to clean her hands, soiled from scrubbing.

Chun Bok was putting rice bran into an oak-log trough for the ox. His mother called, "Bok, here are clean clothes for you. Please hurry! If you cannot take your mind off the ox, I'd better sell him."

He came out of the shed but pretended to be busy pulling weeds in the garden patch.

Omanee's neck flushed with annoyance. "Don't you have ears?"

Keeping his face turned from her, he raised his voice. "I don't like to go to school."

She rushed at him and, before Chun Bok could get up to run, laid her firm hand on his shoulder. Dragging him into the house, she scolded frantically, "Don't you know school is good for you? At your age you can't read or write!"

She picked up a measuring stick, but he still refused stubbornly. "Oma, I will do anything else you say, but I will not go to school."

She brought the stick down again and again on his shoulders, back and thighs, while he vainly pleaded, "Oma, stop!"

Wriggling out of her grasp, he cried out, calling his dead father, "Abuji, please come, help me!"

Omanee dropped the stick, stood silent a moment, then burst into tears. Through his tears, Chun Bok looked at his weeping mother. When he realized that this was the first time she had ever cried in front of him, he cried all the harder. Finally he wiped his tears away with his sleeves, blew his nose loudly, and slowly began to put on fresh clothes of fine woven hemp and the new straw shoes.

Chun Bok, sniffling, followed his mother. They walked silently along the path through the rice paddy. Omanee often turned back to call Chun Bok. "Come on, student."

They entered a trail that wound upward through acacia trees to the sloping edge of the schoolyard. A sea wind working in the branches of the cherry trees sent down a small rain of pink blossoms all over the yard. A girl was gathering petals to make a garland like the one she already wore around her neck. She looked up, and her clear, long-lashed eyes calmly watched the approach of mother and son. A few soft petals had fallen on her dark hair.

Omanee asked, "Young girl, where is your teacher?"

For answer, the girl shook out her skirtful of petals and ran to the schoolhouse. Immediately the windows were filled with wide-eyed faces.

The girl came back with the teacher, a narrow-faced young man in glasses, busily shaking chalk powder off his clothing.

Omanee bowed to the teacher gracefully. He bowed in return, smiled, and said, "You chose a good time to visit us."

Omanee pushed Chun Bok forward. "Don't you bow to the teacher?"

Chun Bok greeted him with a slight bow, but avoided looking directly at him.

"We moved to Lower Valley yesterday," said Omanee.

"Our Butterfly Valley is a good place to live," the teacher nodded. "An ancient poet saw this hill on which the school stands as the body of a giant butterfly and the upper and lower valleys as its wings."

"Will you please make a good person out of this green boy?" asked Omanee.

The teacher said, "We already have thirty-six boys and girls, so we do not have a desk and chair for your son. At the Upper Valley there is a good carpenter who makes a desk and chair for seventy *won*."

Chun Bok did not want to sit on the floor while the other children had desks and chairs. He caught his mother's worried look, and feared she would embarrass him with bargaining. But his mother said, "Get him a desk and chair, please. I will pay you before Tano Day."

The teacher invited her to look around the school farm. "My pupils raise chickens, rabbits, and pigs too."

She said politely, "I must hurry to return to my new house." Then, watching Chun Bok proudly, she added, "He will love to see them. We have an ox at home."

The teacher reached a hand to Chun Bok. When he smiled, his glasses seemed to hide even more of his narrow face. "A girl student is absent today. You may sit in her seat."

Turning, with eyes lowered, Chun Bok walked to the schoolroom.

❀ 3 ❀

WHENEVER Chun Bok felt the boys staring at
him, his eyes turned as if of their own will to the
mountain outside the glass window. He wished he
had gone to the mountain with his ox. The teacher
called him often to face toward him and look at his
pointer traveling among difficult characters or maps
chalked on the blackboard. But Chun Bok longed
for the freedom of the swallows that sometimes flew
inside the schoolroom. They were restless and unhappy before the stares of wild dark-eyed boys until
once again they found the open door.

At recess, away from the friendly boys who came
to play with him, he would go to the school barn in
the backyard. There were pigs enclosed with long

fences, and white rabbits with shiny red eyes in a big cage. He loved to feed the chickens at the far end of the barn, coaxing them nearer and shooing them back from under his feet.

The last period before lunch, the teacher would call for the music lesson. On the organ he played all sorts of tunes. Chun Bok learned that the school had just recently bought the expensive organ. Teacher and students alike had been longing to have one, but the teacher was happiest of all. Over the organ Chun Bok could see only the two gay moons of the teacher's glasses. When he forgot to dismiss the class, some of the pupils stepped out of the room without being dismissed and some in the rear even started to eat their lunch. Then the teacher would announce, "Let's see who brought the best lunch today." Turning to his victim for the day, he would ask, "May I have your lunch today? One of your friends will be glad to share his lunch with you."

One day when lessons had been brief and the music period prolonged with repeated rendering of a song of his own words and composition, "The Wandering Circus Boy," the teacher smiled ingratiatingly at Chun Bok. "Let's see who has a good lunch today.

Chun Bok, I think I will have yours. You may eat with one of the other boys."

Chun Bok surrendered the lunch, but was too shy to wait for anyone who might offer to share his lunch. He strolled from the school grounds to where he had left his ox that morning. He found the animal nibbling grass and swatting flies with his switching tail. Chun Bok let him drink from the stream while he sat on the bank and felt hungry for the delicious scorched rice his mother usually left for his after-school lunch. It was probably waiting at home for him, still in the abalone shell with which she had scraped it from the pot.

He flung himself down on the bank and held on to a large rock with one hand while he drank from the cool flowing water. When he lifted his head, he saw his face mirrored in the stream and another moving small reflection beyond it. He turned and saw the class monitor, panting with haste, her aluminum lunch box in the crook of her arm. She was the one who had been making cherry-petal garlands and brought the teacher to him and his mother on the first day.

"I have been looking for you. Then I saw your big

ox." Dropping beside him on the grass, she held out her lunch box. "We will eat together."

Chun Bok was pleased but could think of nothing to say. She said, "Everyone calls me 'Monitor' but my name is Jung Lan. When someone disappears from the class, the teacher always asks me where he is."

She gazed into his blue eyes and smiled as though just discovering them. Chun Bok, red-faced, blinked dizzily and turned toward his ox.

Jung Lan admired, "I've never seen such a big ox."

She opened her small lunch box and handed her brass chopsticks to Chun Bok. The lunch box yielded white rice and chopped eggs. Jung Lan said, "You see, the teacher does his own cooking. He often takes my lunch. When I tell my mother about it, she always laughs and tells me that it is good to give a meal to the teacher."

The two, handing the chopsticks back and forth to each other, took mouthfuls in turn. Chun Bok tried not to eat much.

"Is the rice too soggy for you?" asked Jung Lan. "My grandmother likes her rice soggy, but I like mine fluffy. I love the scorched parts."

Someday he would bring the scorched rice in the abalone shell to Jung Lan.

Finally there was only a piece of chopped egg. Both of them eyed it. "You had better eat it," she offered.

"No, you should finish the egg."

Neither would give in, so they agreed to give it to the ox. When the large square-jawed animal licked the small bit of food from Chun Bok's palm, Jung Lan giggled so loud that the ox was startled.

The school bell was ringing. "Let's run to school," she said.

Chun Bok tethered his ox slowly, wishing he could stay with his animal.

"Oh, come on," urged Jung Lan. "Tardy ones have to wipe up the floor."

"Isn't today your turn to clean?"

"Yes."

"I am good at cleaning. I'll help you, Jung Lan."

They hurried back to school, her legs skipping to keep up with his long strides. Chun Bok was feeling that school life was not bad.

In the class, the teacher brought out a big picture book and announced, "I will now show you a circus."

They shouted in glee and piled up before the teacher. Chun Bok stood behind the eager boys and watched each colorful page that the teacher turned: elephants dancing, lions obeying their trainer, some odd-looking animals with stripes, and then the circus parade. These were very different from the dog-and-monkey circus Chun Bok had seen on the island. In his mind Chun Bok was already describing the strange pictures to Omanee.

While showing the pictures of circus animals, the teacher imitated their noises. The bobbed heads and pigtails before Chun Bok shook with laughter. A small girl nearest the teacher stood up, trying to touch the picture of a camel.

The teacher held the book high to his ear and showed the next picture, a pink, funny-looking man. His big nose reached from his narrow forehead almost to his laughing mouth. The absorbed flat faces of the boys and girls rounded into giggles as they moved closer to the picture, some exclaiming, "The circus boy!" The teacher remarked, "It is a clown."

"Clown" kept coming from their mouths, echoing with wonder. The teacher explained, "You see, a clown has a big nose, twice as large as yours, and he can fill his great big mouth, and fills yours too, with laughter. His eyes — let me see." The teacher's face turned to the picture he was holding.

"The circus boy — I mean the clown's eyes are crying!" A girl raised her voice sadly.

"No, they are laughing." Many began to argue, but the class became quiet again when the teacher went on, "They look different, yes, and a bit bewildered, and if you come too close to look into them, they seem to look the other way like a bird's eyes."

Chun Bok feared someone might turn around to point at his eyes, and he lowered his face.

The teacher's free hand picked up a pencil, and raising it high, he said, "Let's sing." They opened their mouths wide for "The Wandering Circus Boy." They sang the slow sad song loudly and happily.

The teacher rushed to the new organ and the music class started again:

When we returned next day
He was gone —
That circus boy was gone.
Let's sing with crickets,
Let's sing with green frogs,
Till he returns.

After school Chun Bok stayed inside to help the girls at cleaning up the classroom. On the playground, a soccer ball was bouncing back and forth, the boys running after it. As he was leaving the school to go home, a boy called him to join the game.

Jung Lan and some of the other girls returned from the well, where they had been washing their feet after the cleaning, and stopped to watch the boys play.

Many of the children wore rubber shoes, some tennis shoes. A player dashed forward, stopped the flying ball with his bulging forehead, and kicked it far with his squeaking shoes. Chun Bok was conscious of his straw shoes. But he ran with all his might, and, when the ball rolled to him, kicked it with all his strength. One of his shoes flew off, outdistanced the ball, and landed in the midst of the girls under the cherry tree. He had to hop on one foot to get it. The girls giggled and the boys laughed loudly.

Chun Bok flushed red. As he hastily put on his shoe, he heard someone shout, "Bird Eye didn't aim right!"

He felt as though cold water had been poured over

his head. He did not return to the game. His new friends had begun to ridicule his eyes. The girls were gone now from the cherry tree, but he knew that Jung Lan had heard the taunt.

The boy in squeaking shoes grabbed the ball and announced that he was going home. The other boys in protest made a circle around the owner of the ball. "Pal Min, let's play a little longer," a few asked.

Pal Min, putting on his coat, called to Chun Bok, standing aloof. "Bird Eye, come here!"

Pal Min drew a package from a pocket of his black serge coat. The boys went to the back of the school-house. Chun Bok followed slowly, wondering what would happen.

Opening a paper of saccharin, the boy in squeaking shoes declared, "This is a thousand times sweeter than sugar. I can make ten gourds of water sweet with just this little bit."

Like a magician, he dropped a tiny portion of the white powder into the gourd of water. He offered it to one of the boys, who drank about half and passed it to another to finish. Chun Bok took his turn with the rest. No one wanted more.

"Who can drink the most sweet water?" challenged Pal Min.

Several boys promptly accepted the dare, but no one could finish so much as a gourdful.

"How much can you drink, Bird Eye?" demanded the swaggering boy in squeaking shoes. He was surprised when Chun Bok seized the gourd and downed all the sickening contents.

Another gourdful went the way of the first, and there were a third and a fourth. Chun Bok was panting when he had finished the fifth portion, but he was happy to see that his feat had amazed his playmates. No one called him Bird Eye then.

Satisfied with himself, Chun Bok strutted slowly down to the stream where his ox was grazing. He started home, leading his animal, but soon began to feel the water sloshing around inside him. With every step he felt worse.

He had no appetite for his evening meal. "I have a pain in my side," he told his anxious mother. "I think I drank too much water at school."

He went to lie down, and tossed and groaned in his quilt. Omanee called in her neighbor. The old farmer's wife came over, clicking her tongue in pity. "There is no medicine for sickness from drinking water. Wait till morning and give him mugwort juice."

Chun Bok was not able to sleep well. He felt too warm, and kicked off the cover. His mother stayed up all night and rubbed him wherever he felt a pain and spread the cover over him. Every time he awoke, he met Omanee's worried blue eyes watching him. There was comfort in Omanee's care.

At the first crow of a rooster in the Lower Valley, she stole out of the house to gather dewy mugwort, from which she ground half a bowl of juice. Holding the bowl lightly in both hands, she turned to him, praying, "May this bowl cure my son, and may the sunrise find my son no longer ill."

Then she put her arm around him. "Bok, drink this."

"No, no. I will not!"

"This is honey water," she urged, pouring a spoonful of honey into the bitter juice in the bowl.

Chun Bok conquered a moment of queasiness. He drank it all and licked his lips. She tucked the quilt over him and he went to sleep.

❁ *4* ❁

THE morning light was filtering through the paper windows when his mother's hand tested the fever in his forehead. Chun Bok was much better and could get up to take rice soup.

However, Chun Bok did not feel well enough to go to school, nor did he want to go. Omanee said nothing about school even when Chun Bok went with her to buy earthen jars for raising bean sprouts.

They passed a group of houses whose leaning roofs seemed to be supporting one another, and came to the big shady oak where several old men gathered. Beyond them sat large and small earthen jars with ears on them. Among the old men Chun Bok saw the neighboring farmer weaving straw shoes, and he bowed to him. The farmer had laid aside a half-woven shoe to fill his pipe. He acknowledged Chun Bok's bow happily and said, "You look well now. I heard you were sick from drinking too much water."

Beside the neighbor two older men faced each other across a checkerboard. They sat cross-legged on small mats, their backs erect, their eyes on the game. One, with a checker poised in one hand, used the other hand to keep his full sleeve from sweeping the board. His silvery hair blew softly from under his horsehair hat. Very slowly, he asked, "Did he really drink too much water and get sick?"

Turning to the man in the horsehair hat, the old neighbor commented, "This boy shows respect for elderly men." Then he said, "Will you take his pulse?"

Still keeping his eyes on the game, the man in the horsehair hat clasped Chun Bok's wrist. Between moves on the board he announced, "This boy's pulse is regular and unusually strong. He is all right."

Omanee stepped forward and bowed slightly. "I am grateful, elderly man."

"But after sickness," the old man went on, "one should be extra careful and stay at home quietly for a while. In the old times we used budding horns of deer and ginseng for good remedies."

The neighbor farmer interrupted the herb man's talk by telling Omanee, "Don't wait for the jar maker. Pay him when you meet later." He began to weave shoes again.

Omanee went to the earthen jars and picked two brown ones of different sizes. The other checker player lowered his glasses to the tip of his nose and asked Chun Bok, "Do you go to school?"

Chun Bok did not answer. He lowered his eyes and kicked the ground with his straw shoe. His mother said from behind the oak tree, "Yes, elderly man." Then she added worriedly, gazing at the glow on one of the jars, "But he would rather stay with his ox than go to school."

"I am not a frog in a pond," the herb man declared, watching the mother's face to note the effect of his words. "I have walked all over the country selling my ginseng herb. The island you came from produces a fine stock of oxen. Don't hurry him to start school. Let your boy take your ox to the mountain for the lush green grass and the spring sun, Chun Bok's mother. This queer education — singing, running — everything they do is emptying stomachs which their parents have to fill."

The checker player with glasses advised, "We built our muscles by chopping wood and helping our parents. These young children do not know any practical matter but run without knowing why."

The high-pitched singing of the schoolchildren was heard from the school. The old man shook his head. "See, they sing all the time and never have quiet moments to learn. Chun Bok's mother, if your boy doesn't want to go, send him to us; we will teach him old wisdom and proverbs."

"Stay in peace, elderly men," said Omanee.

As she and Chun Bok left, each carrying a jar, an argument broke out between the checker players as to where the game had left off.

Back at the house, Omanee took the two jars to the room, the smaller to hold bean seeds and the larger to hold water. The bean jar was set upon bamboo sticks across the rim of the water jar. Omanee dipped up water with her small gourd dipper and poured it over the seeds again and again. She showed Chun Bok small holes in the bottom of the jar from which the water tinkled back down to the outer jar and said, "You may scoop the water to use over and over again to wet the bean seeds."

After placing the jars in a dark corner of the room, Omanee said, "Bok, you should raise bean sprouts, for I have to be out all day, selling the seaweed we brought from the island to meet your school fee. It is true that bean sprouts bring only a small price, but it takes little money to grow them, and everybody eats bean sprouts."

Chun Bok thought it fun to water sprouts and to see them growing.

Realizing his ox must be hungry and restless, he went to the barn. He gave the ox an unusually large feeding of rice bran in the trough, added a tubful of water, then more rice bran. Watching his ox's large black eyes, Chun Bok wondered what the ox thought about his blue eyes.

❁ 5 ❁

CHUN BOK rested all day and in the late afternoon set out with his ox for the mountain. Two tiger butterflies flitted over the shallow ditch along his way. Two others followed a man who was approaching; in his wooden carrying frame he had a load of grass roots, weeds and blooming plants. Noticing edible plants, Chun Bok thought that the man's jars of grain must be getting low in the hard times before the barley harvest.

As they met, Chun Bok heard him saying to himself, "Schoolchildren are out. The day must be coming to a close." He squinted at the sun over West Mountain.

Chun Bok looked more closely at the contents of

the carrying frame. "A big arrowroot!" he exclaimed.

The man set his nail-tipped stick into the ground as partial support for the carrying frame. "Schoolboy, I will give you some to chew on your way," he said. "Don't let your ox go to others' grain patches."

Chun Bok respectfully received the bite-sized slice with both his hands. He was too pleased to thank him aloud.

As the man passed on, Chun Bok walked faster and more cheerfully, the ox at his heels. His jaws moved in time with his steps, and feeling warm, he untied the two gray cords of his topcoat.

At the foot of the mountain old tombs lay scattered. Lower branches of a pear tree touched lightly a broken tombstone. Behind the pear blossoms, someone cried out, "Wha!"

Chun Bok dropped the halter he held. The ox let out a low "Oome, oome!"

Jung Lan came up suddenly before him, her shoulders shaking with laughter. She carried a bamboo basket full of tender leaves of mulberries.

Chun Bok offered the remaining arrowroot. "It is very sappy," he said. "If you chew long enough there won't be any fiber left."

Jung Lan pointed at Chun Bok's mouth. "Look at

the gray ring around your lips. I see you have chewed the root all day like your ox and forgotten to come to school."

Chun Bok started to wipe his lips with the back of his hand.

"Why don't you come to school?" she asked seriously.

"I don't like to go to school."

"But why? School is very nice."

He said nothing about being called "Bird Eye." "In school I saw that all the boys wore tennis shoes or rubber shoes."

"Why don't you tell your mother to buy you some shoes like the rest have?" Her eyes were diverted to his shoes and his ox's hooves. "Even many cows no longer wear straw shoes."

"My Oma doesn't spend much money. She is saving until she has a great deal."

Looking sorry for Chun Bok, Jung Lan pondered aloud, "I will talk to my class to see if we can help you get a pair of tennis shoes."

"No, no, my Oma wouldn't like it at all," Chun Bok said.

Jung Lan abruptly turned toward the shadowed green ricefields down in the valley. "I must give supper to my silkworms and prepare my own." She walked away rapidly, swinging her free hand.

Somewhere near, a mockingbird chirped, and Chun Bok threw a stone bitterly and angrily in the direction of the unseen bird.

❀ 6 ❀

ON the following morning Chun Bok did not get up when his mother called him. He had decided to pretend to still be ill. After Omanee left to peddle the seaweed he finally came out of the room. The shadow of the house had lifted from the patch of peppers. Sunlight was on the ox's brown back in the shed. Sitting on the porch, Chun Bok ate his breakfast alone — the mixture of cooked rice and barley, eggplant stew and pickled cabbage.

Then he set out for the mountain to collect pine knots for fuel and graze his ox. On the way he stopped by the great oak and heard the old men recount their stories and sayings. He did not come down from the mountain till the supper smoke time, when green frogs croaked alone in the darkening ricefields.

At home he left the ox and the burlap sack of pine knots and dry branches in the shed and went to the kitchen, where his mother was preparing supper. He put one foot on the old gray log at the entrance and stood without calling her. With her sleeves rolled up to the middle of her forearms, she was busy among the jars. Seeing him, she exclaimed in relief, "Why, Bok, what have you been doing all day?"

Chun Bok turned slightly to avoid the reprimand in her eyes and stood still. She asked gently, "What did the old men teach you? Can you repeat anything they told you?" His mother spoke again. "Just a few words to please your mother, Bok."

With downcast eyes, he recited shorter sayings the old man in the horsehair hat had told him: " 'A robber runs away from his own footsounds.' 'One cannot spit on a smiling face.' 'A blind man steals eggs his own hens have laid.' "

Omanee smiled and said, "Like farmers here, we ought to raise chickens. You will help me fence around the kitchen garden to protect vegetables from pecking beaks."

When Chun Bok did not respond to her plan, Omanee seemed to search him. "Did you have a fight with anyone?" she asked.

"No, Oma," he answered simply.

She dropped her eyes and did not question him further. She said musingly, as though recalling her island days, "In my forty years, I have never seen two abalones of the same size, shape and color. It is the same with human beings." She took out pickled cabbage from a jar, and taking off the lid of the jar of hot pepper sauce, she continued slowly, "Even when there are twins or triplets in a family, they are never quite the same. It is blue in the seed that makes ours different from others'."

He wanted even more than before to ask why he did not take after the dark in his father's seed, but words did not come from his mouth. He merely watched Omanee moving about in the kitchen. She stooped down to the pit under the kettle, and blew with her strong long breath. When a flare rose like a candle, she turned her face away from the smoke. Her blue eyes watered, reflecting the fire. She said unhappily, "Don't stand there like that. You keep the smoke from going out."

Chun Bok went to the stream and washed his hands. Holding his hands before him to dry in the air, he watched the dark water making an eddy at the bend and flowing over tiny pebbles. He stayed until his mother called him.

❀ 7 ❀

CHUN BOK stayed late in his room every morning till he was certain that the time to go to school was well past. He often felt heavy-headed and drowsy, and faintly remembered his sleep had been interrupted by nightmares.

Raising her voice higher so as to be heard by the neighbors, Omanee would call again, "Still you don't wake up?"

He would answer, "I am awake but too weak to go to school," and doze off again.

After Omanee had left home, the old neighbor would call him over to the fence to tell him some proverbs. "If you go through the village in early morning looking for doors already open you can pick out the homes that will prosper." "A wise crab goes out alone into the ocean rather than staying on the dry sand pitying himself with his bubbles."

Chun Bok did not leave the house except to go to the mountain pasture to graze his ox. He often watered the growing bean sprouts and enjoyed watching the first shoots turning pale and tender. He was mystified at how rapidly they grew in the shade on water alone.

Shortly after returning home, Omanee would light the kerosene lamp bright to see the bean sprouts. One evening, two days before Tano Day, Omanee said happily, "These beans have already grown. I can sell them soon."

Chun Bok, hanging over the jar, asked, "Oma, how do the dry hard beans become such yellow-capped shoots?"

Omanee had no real answer. "They just do," she said. "There is something in the seed that tells it to be a bean sprout."

On the day after Omanee took the last portion of the seaweed to peddle from door to door, Chun Bok hoed the pepper plant patch along his neighbor's fence. Someone called from behind, "Chun Bok." It was Jung Lan. He stood up to welcome her, but could not meet her friendly eyes.

Jung Lan extended a small clenched fist. "What do you think I have in my hand?"

Before he could answer she spread out her fingers, showing three pieces of silver money. She had been holding the coins so tightly that her little palms carried the marks of money.

Chun Bok could not help showing his surprise. "Oh, that is real money!"

"It is for you," said the girl solemnly. "You can buy tennis shoes and come to school again."

He withdrew his hand, refusing. "Where did you get those silver coins?" asked Chun Bok, avoiding her eyes.

She explained proudly, "I told the class why you didn't want to come to school. Everyone raising chickens at home gave an egg for your new pair of shoes. One boy carried an egg in his pocket, and finding it broken when he reached the school, he cried and cried." Chun Bok wished Jung Lan would talk in low tones for fear his neighbors might hear, but she went on cheerfully. "You know Pal Min from the rich tile-roofed house? He surprised us at school by taking out an egg from every pocket of his Western coat and trousers — altogether six large eggs.

"This morning we took those eggs to the top of the slope. One of the women on her way to the holiday market bought them and gave me the silver money. Everyone wanted to come to present the money to you, but I told them you wouldn't like to receive the gift before so many."

Chun Bok, with his hands still behind his back, refused to accept the coins. Bewildered, he watched Jung Lan putting the coins on the porch. She walked to the gate, then turned back to say, "I will tell the class that you are going to the Harbor Town to buy tennis shoes and will come to school tomorrow and the day after tomorrow. We will go to Pestle to swing and to see many holiday events."

Chun Bok stood for a long time watching the empty road beyond the fence. Then he slowly walked to the stream to wash the old grubby hoe which he was still carrying in his hand. While carefully washing its worn blade, he said aloud as if the old hoe had ears, "If only I had dark eyes!"

At the other end of the stream an unmoving bullfrog sat facing Chun Bok. Its breathing swelled its white breast and rippled the water. Chun Bok sat still, staring at the frog's pealike eyes, until it jumped from his sight.

❀ *8* ❀

IN the afternoon Chun Bok attached the small bells to the ox's collar and started for the Harbor Town. At the great oak he passed the old men without talking, but the neighbor farmer called out, "Come here, Chun Bok. Where are you going?"

Chun Bok turned back to greet him. "I am going to the market."

"With your ox? Why?" the neighbor asked. "Before the ox match on Tano Day, farmers would break their heads to borrow or buy your fine animal. Leave him on the mountain for grazing."

An old man from the Upper Valley turned to the herb man and asked, "What caused the lad to have a different eye color?"

The herb man seemed to weigh the matter. "He was born delicate and has never had the right medicine. If he could have plenty of real Korean ginseng and the budding horn of a fawn for a month, he would be all right. The good medicines are hard to find today."

"But he is bigger than other boys of his age. He cannot be weak," the Upper Valley man disagreed.

Chun Bok waited for a break in the conversation to leave. But the herb doctor turned to him to tell a story. "My grandfather told me a tale about a blue-eyed sailor from across the blue water and blue mountains who drifted to the island after a typhoon and caught the loving eyes of a diver. The island people drove this couple out of the village, and the lovers went up to the high mountain to live as husband and wife. They lived on wild grass until they tired of it. One day the diver found a pumpkin seed in her clothes bundle and planted it. It grew into an immense vine, and after that they lived on pumpkins happily."

"That man's eyes were blue," the Upper Valley man said, gazing at Chun Bok's eyes.

The checker player in his horn-rimmed glasses said, "One eye of mine is much bigger than the other, so I was unhappy in my childhood. Since I started wearing glasses, no one seems to notice the different sizes." He lowered his glasses to the tip of his nose to look at Chun Bok closely. "This lad is strong and lively and has a full tight mouth and jaw. I like him."

The herb doctor said to Chun Bok, "Don't lend your ox to anyone before Tano Day. He might join the ox match with him. If your animal got hurt, no one would hire him to plow land."

Chun Bok left quietly as the old men started a round of wine. While climbing the mountain he fancied himself becoming a cattleman and always being with oxen. Even the old men were curious about his blue eyes. He wanted to stay away from everyone.

Chun Bok took his ox to pasture and started for the Harbor Town across the mountain. He disliked taking the money from his school friends. How could he explain to his mother about the pair of tennis shoes he was to buy in town? He wished that they had jeered, teased or even bullied him so he could hit them, hit them again, until they would not dare to come close to him. But unlike the island children, they were so friendly that he could not fight with them. "One cannot spit on a smiling face" — he remembered the old saying. He was sure of only one thing; he hated being called "Bird Eye" as much as he had hated being called "Fish Eye."

From the bridge that led to the main road to the harbor, Chun Bok was more and more uncertain whether he should continue. His mind was whirling.

The road was busy with market-bound people. Oxen passed led by farmers. Bicycle riders dodged women with baskets on their heads. On the other side of the road many brown cows and oxen were being driven along. He slowed down watching a group of animals and their calves huddled together only a tail's distance from each other. When a car honked from behind, Chun Bok ran startled to the edge of the road, almost colliding with a small boy in a buttoned-up uniform. The boy was wearing glasses under his school cap.

Remembering what one of the old men under the oak tree had said, he thought aloud, "If I wear glasses, people won't see the color of my eyes." Each time he saw someone with glasses he was reassured and walked faster toward the market.

Along the shore road the windows of the pottery, china and lacquerware shops glittered in the afternoon sun. He passed by a shoe store but did not stop. Instead, he gazed at the display of sunglasses in a nearby stall. He lingered, watching and thinking, for a long time. Slowly he reached for a pair of dark glasses that would conceal his blue eyes. His hands trembled as he put them on. Feeling as though the sun had hidden behind a dark cloud, he raised his chin toward the stall mirror. An odd-looking face with dark-framed glasses peered at him from the mirror. Chun Bok moved closer. Wide dark eyes framed in a pale sadness stared at him curiously and awkwardly. He felt strange, yet protected, as though in the evening.

Chun Bok paid for the glasses with the silver coins and walked toward the pier, watching his reflection in the store windows. He put his glasses in his pocket and walked around the bay till his shadow grew large walking beside him. Tired and worried, he crouched down and faced the flickering of the lamp in the distant lighthouse. He imagined the hurt look that would come into Omanee's blue eyes if she should find out about the glasses. But without this protection he could not look his school friends in their faces. His thought of wearing the glasses to go to school went on and off like the lighthouse.

Finally he got up to go home. "No, I won't show

the glasses to Omanee, but in school I will wear them; then no one will call me 'Bird Eye.' " As though touching his deep secret, his hand ran timidly over his bulging pocket.

❀ *9* ❀

IN the early morning Chun Bok told Omanee that he would go to school today. She breathed deeply and happily. "From now on I can breathe unworried." Then she gave him seventy *won* to give the teacher for the desk and chair.

After breakfast, Omanee picked the long sprouts from the jar tenderly and placed them in her market basket. She said, "As tomorrow is Tano, luck may be ahead of me in today's market. Then I will have enough money to buy white rice, fish and good vegetables to celebrate the big holiday and your schooling all at once."

"After school I will bring the ox to the market to carry the rice," Chun Bok said.

She nodded, smiling, and put a thick pad of cloth on her head to soften the pressure of the load of bean sprouts. With the basket shaped to her head by its weight, Omanee walked light-footed and briskly.

Chun Bok's hands trembled on the halter as he led his ox out of the shed. The animal would graze on the bank of the stream near the school grounds where he and Jung Lan had had the delicious lunch. Once out of his yard, he looked about to make sure that there was no one around. Then he put the sunglasses on, resting the black stems over his ears. The rice-fields seemed to become underwater weeds. Feeling timid and awkward, he walked behind his ox, his face downward as though confronting rough wind. Along the way his ox halted to munch grass. He stooped over a ricefield pond to study his dim reflection till his eyelids smarted painfully with uncried tears.

As he saw the school from the acacia trail, his feet moved more slowly and heavily. Girls were playing marbles at the edge of the playground. One girl saw him, then all of them stopped playing and, holding the marbles in their hands, stared at him. Slowing down his steps further, he found three boys at one of the cherry trees looking at him and laughing; another was shading his eyes against the morning sun with his school bundle. Cold sweat broke out on Chun Bok's forehead.

Without knowing exactly why, he turned back and took a narrow path away from the school — across the buckwheat field. He took off his sunglasses and walked unseeingly as if on a night road.

Chun Bok did not realize how long he and his ox had wandered the mountains when he found himself near the bridge. Stopping in the warm noon shadow of his ox, he wondered whether he should go on to meet his mother in the market. A flowing current combed through the willow branches and outlined the rail of the wooden bridge as he and the ox walked over it. With the market-bound people, he went on beyond the bridge, still undecided. The gay voices of the farmers and mooings of the cattle rose from the cattle market. He wanted to see those tan, chestnut, small and big animals.

With many onlookers men haggled gaily over prices. Vendors also moved around with taffy, sweet potatoes, fruits. Chun Bok's ox threw his big head from side to side restlessly and pulled on his halter.

No sooner had Chun Bok entered the cattle market than a ragged fellow plucked him by the sleeve. "You will sell this for two thousand."

Before Chun Bok could refuse, another heavy voice raised the price: "Two and a half thousand?"

The gnarled fingers of still another farmer already lay on the heavy shoulder of the ox. "Three thousand?"

As rough buyers started to surround him, he quickly tapped the sleek rump of his ox to move away. One snorted, "The small rascal is merely amusing himself by bringing his ox here!"

Leading his ox close to the edge of the market boardering on the ricefield terraces, he watched other animals from afar. "Boy," someone called loudly, "do you want to have your ox shod?"

Chun Bok turned. A heavy-set man was squatting alone by a bare apricot tree. He was wearing dirty trousers with black patches on the knees. On a reed mattress behind the man were laid metal strips, chains and other tools. When Chun Bok did not answer, he came over, talking coaxingly. "Come on, boy. You know, straw shoes last like straw, and iron ones last like iron."

"How much is it?" Chun Bok was curious.

"Ninety *won*," said the man.

He was surprised by his thought of getting his ox iron shoes.

"What about seventy?" His tone of voice was now serious, haggling.

With a contemptuous grunt, the man turned his back to Chun Bok and puffed his short-stemmed pipe.

Chun Bok lingered, unable to make himself leave. He watched the hooves of other animals led by farmers. There were more oxen shod with iron than with twisted straw.

The cattle-shoe man came over to Chun Bok again. "Have you got all the money with you?" he asked.

Chun Bok instantly reached into his pocket and presented the money.

The man bound the ox's legs with a chain. The ox bellowed as his low knee joints were tied and pulled together to cause him to fall. The huge animal hit the ground, his hooves churning the air. He struggled to get up, his eyes swimming with fear. Chun Bok's jaw quivered violently as the ox's huge body rose up and down.

The shoe man unmindfully went on tightening

the chain that had already intertwined around the legs, and started to work fast. He used every tool on the mattress.

The ox, finally subdued, no longer mooed but often jerked. Chun Bok watched fascinated as the shoe man attached a metal strip to each hoof and studded in the round nails swiftly.

The cattle-shoe man finished his work and unbound the chain from the legs, but the ox still lay on the ground. Chun Bok, laughing, tugged at the square head and got him up.

The man whisked off a towel from his cloth belt and with it wiped his sweaty neck. "Are you going to join the ox fight tomorrow? Some of the oxen here will go there to fight."

"No, he might get hurt. I don't want to see my ox fight."

The man tapped dust off the low belly of the animal. "Can any ox be better fed than this one? Just the right ox for a winning match. Where are you from, boy?"

"My mother and I moved to Butterfly Valley from Cheju Island," Chun Bok answered.

"Cheju! As far as that!" He peered at Chun Bok

closely. "Are there many blue-eyed people there?" he asked.

Chun Bok lowered his face and without further delay pulled the halter to leave. At first the ox moved limpingly as though sore-footed, but soon the iron-shod hooves fell on the pebbly road lightly and comfortably.

❀ *10* ❀

CHUN BOK took his ox to the sea to give him a rubdown. It was ebb tide; a few boats were anchored far out in the sea. Sunlight glinted on the waves.

"There he is!" shouted someone.

A group of boys and girls were standing in front of his house. The boys were jumping down the sea wall toward him. Chun Bok pulled his ox out to get away from them. The shadows of their heads already rushed upon him. "Bird Eye," a shrill voice cried, "you can't fly away after taking our eggs." The shouts of the boys filled his ears.

Realizing it was too late to run away, Chun Bok shivered, his face covered with fright-flesh. The boys slowed down as the shore mud clung to their shoes. Chun Bok took the glasses from his pocket and slipped them on rapidly. The boys halted five or six steps from him, stamping their muddy shoes. They formed a crescent. Chun Bok's ox turned his head toward them cautiously, then dropped it to go behind Chun Bok. Pal Min lifted his shoulders and stepped out of the group. He thrust out his big lower lip as his gaze moved from Chun Bok's sunglasses to his straw shoes, and again back to the sunglasses. "Beat him flat, Pal Min, until everything he ate comes out!" A plump boy pushed Pal Min forward. "He must have spent our egg money for candy and pumpkin pancakes."

"He must have bought those funny-looking glasses with the money." Another shook his fist at Chun Bok.

Pal Min's bulging forehead lowered in a motion of butting Chun Bok. Chun Bok, startled, raised the crook of his arm. The boys laughed. Pal Min demanded, "Take the glasses off your bird eyes." Chun Bok bit his lips, not moving.

Pal Min shook his head threateningly like an angry ox. Chun Bok stepped back, raising the crook of his arm again. The boys laughed again. Pal Min repeated his demand: "Bird Eye, take off your glasses."

Chun Bok gripped his ox's halter tight. Suddenly Pal Min's forefinger poked at Chun Bok's nose. The glasses fell off and dropped before him. Pal Min kicked the glasses away with his squeaking shoe. Chun Bok blinked and wavered, turning his face away from the boys' staring eyes.

Pal Min grabbed him by the collar. "I'll break your neck if you keep turning away from us." He shook Chun Bok, demanding, "Look at me and squawk something, Bird Eye, will you?"

Chun Bok turned his head farther away, still holding the halter.

An anguished gasp came from behind the boys. It was Jung Lan and some of the other girls. "Pal Min, you are choking him. Don't! Please don't!" she said frantically.

Pal Min did not look at her. "You told us to bring eggs. You shouldn't have listened to this island brat."

A lanky boy raised his thin arm. "Bird Eye never looks at us, he's never friendly. Pal Min, give a good blow to the island fellow."

Another boy in mud-spotted trousers piped in, "Teacher said a dishonest man doesn't look others in the eye, remember? He has something to hide."

"Liar!" "Bird Eye!" Others circled close to Chun Bok and Pal Min.

Chun Bok turned his pale, tense face to Pal Min. He asked bitterly, "Why do you care if my eyes are not the same color as yours?" He could not keep his voice from trembling.

"What? What did you say?" Pal Min asked, pulling at Chun Bok's collar. Then he loosened his grip, apparently groping for an answer.

"Because ours are human color!" one of the other boys called. "Yours are bird eyes."

"Let's give this liar as many blows as those eggs he got," the one in the mud-spotted trousers proposed.

Another responded, "Pal Min, you give him six blows, for you gave Bird Eye six eggs." Then he threw out his fist and hit Chun Bok on the cheek. Another fist landed on the side of his head. Chun Bok staggered and would have fallen had he not held the halter. The ox, puzzled by the sudden jerk, watched the boys closely.

Recovered from the surprise and force of the blows, Chun Bok stepped back, lowering his chin. Pal Min moved in, raising his fist. Chun Bok nimbly evaded him and punched hard at Pal Min's chin.

Others grabbed Chun Bok, jabbing at his head and face, then toward his chest and stomach.

For a moment blackness hung over him; he spread his legs wider so as not to fall. Halfway to his knees on the mud flat he took one weak step. His hand touched his nose and he felt blood. He struggled to his feet, bitter anger burning in his blue eyes. He ran to one side and grabbed a large stone to throw at them. Everyone scattered except the girls. The ox pulled back and mooed in fright. Jung Lan, weeping, was holding his ox.

Chun Bok, clutching his heavy stone, chased the boys. Pal Min, fleeing, stumbled over a piece of driftwood. Chun Bok caught up with him. Pal Min seized the wood and whirled it to fend off Chun Bok and his rock, then ran as fast as he could. Chun Bok threw the stone with all his might. But the heavy rock landed short of the fleeing boy and splashed in a puddle. Chun Bok picked up the driftwood Pal Min had dropped, lifting it high, dashed after the boys. Around and over the huge rocks they ran.

They came to the bank of a ricefield. The surge of revenge ran wild in his head. If he should catch anyone, he would strike him hard with the wood.

The boys were running between the ricefields. At a tall pine tree they stopped to regroup, then took the upward path that led to school.

Chun Bok followed them on the long, crooked road up, up to the low hill. At the edge of the school grounds the boys watched Chun Bok coming.

Out of breath with his haste, Chun Bok walked, shouting, "Don't you run away, you cowards!"

The boys stood as if they had decided to fight. Chun Bok darted up, flinging the driftwood toward them. They all fled as fast as dogs, some with their hands covering the backs of their heads. Chun Bok went around the school. No one was in sight.

He came to the end of the school barn lot and looked at every corner of the chicken shed. There was no one. In anger, he opened the swinging door so wide that it banged the outside wall. With loud cackling the chickens flew to the sooty ceiling. He entered the shed and stamped his foot to scare the flock out of the shed. The hens flapped their wings and flew into the yard. Eggs rolled on the floor spotted with chicken droppings. Feathers flew. Behind the school building chickens squawked everywhere.

Still no one came out of their hiding places. He

strode to the pigpen and unfastened the rope that held the pen door shut. As he entered the pen, fat pigs, small and large, snouting and grunting, herded in a corner. Chun Bok hit the corner with the driftwood to drive them out. The black pigs ran all over the ground among the white hens.

"Chunk Bok, what are you doing?" Around the corner of the schoolhouse appeared Jung Lan. She was leading his ox.

Chun Bok stood breathing defiantly and watching the loose livestock. Jung Lan dropped the ox's halter and with her arms spread wide ran to stop the herd of pigs. The pigs trotted, scattered and dodged Jung Lan. Soon they gathered again at the edge of the cabbage patch. The ox came to Chun Bok, lifting his head for attention.

On the other side of the cabbage patch appeared several boys. New anger surged up in Chun Bok. He trembled and bit his lips spitefully. Clutching his ox's halter, he walked with big steps toward the herd of pigs. The young swine slipped into the green field below and trampled the vegetables. They plucked at the cabbage patch.

More boys came and darted around the field, their hands clutching stones. Chun Bok again pulled his

ox by the halter to chase the swine farther away. When his ox refused to move, he whipped him with the driftwood. But he released the halter from his hand too late, stumbled and fell into the field as his ox leaped down to the green patch.

The black pigs ran again. The ox halted in the middle of the vegetable field and watched. Then he lowered his head to munch cabbages. The boys pelted stones at the ox. The brown animal scampered across the field to dodge the stones. One hit the ox on his heavy belly, another on his shoulder. The animal threw up his head and swerved. He leaped and dashed out of the green patch and made for the barley, his tail swinging wildly.

Chun Bok ran after the ox but soon had to stop for breath. The sound of running hooves faded at the foot of West Mountain. Chun Bok walked on, calling, "Oome, oome." He peered into the mountain shadows and listened. There was only the sound of wind passing through the pines. On the flat slope of wild grazing grass he called again and again. In the gray dusk he strained his ears but heard only insects and, farther down, green frogs. Walking slowly back, Chun Bok hoped his ox might have returned home and be waiting for him there.

❀ *11* ❀

THE house stood unlighted — no gleam from any part of it. Omanee had not returned from the market. Chun Bok heard his heart beat as he approached the shed. There was no familiar heavy trampling of hooves, not even a stir of straw. He shivered as though he had stayed long in the cold water.

Chun Bok felt, rather than heard, scattered sounds of boys. He dashed to the room and through the cracks at the edges of the window frame looked outside. He saw the teacher, followed by a group of boys, coming toward the yard. In the dim twilight, he could not recognize a single boy. The teacher raised his disturbed voice: "Is there no one at this house?"

Chun Bok did not dare to look. His breathing

stopped as he heard one of the boys saying, "He must be hiding in his room."

"No, we should wait here," the teacher said.

He should go to find his ox, Chun Bok thought, before they came to catch him. How could he explain to his mother what had happened? Without his ox! How could he face her, anyway?

Chun Bok slipped out of the room stealthily. Then he darted to the back of the house and clambered hastily over the waist-high mud fence. He ran, trying not to make footsounds. As he came near the great oak, he saw the approaching figure of a woman carrying a basket on her head. He stepped behind the tree and watched his mother plod by. She steadied her bamboo basket with both hands and its load pressed it close on her head. Omanee must have sold all the sprouts and bought the food for tomorrow's holiday.

He wanted to cry, "Oma!" and dash out to carry her load. But he stayed hidden until her dark erect figure had passed. Then he came out and watched her moving farther and farther from him. How disappointed she would be when she got home and found him and his ox gone!

Chun Bok walked up from the terraced fields to West Mountain. He was frightened by scarecrows dressed in flapping white topcoats. The wind rustled the shadowed branches of the trees scattered on humps and hollows of old tombs. Then he lost the trail and made his way through thorny growths of wild roses and climbed the ledge of the mountain.

Having no heart to go on farther, he dropped down on the top of the hill. High overhead shone the stars. It came over Chun Bok that he was very much alone. Would he be able to find the ox? Where was the ox? He lay down with his head pillowed on his arm, thinking and worrying.

The young moon rose over the gently waving line of the dark mountain. Below and beyond the dark shell-like island dozed on a stretch of silver. The sea was lovelier for being far off. As the sea breeze became cold he slowly rose to search for his ox again.

He walked to the farthest end of the ledge shoulder on the far side of the mountain. A trail appeared to start at a mountain patch of potato planting. Feeling a stomach that had had no supper, he dug out tubers, some the size of his thumb, some the size of his fist. Sitting on an uprooted tree nearby, he ate the raw potatoes greedily. His hunger eased, he looked about. Not far from him, some vines were trampled and stripped of leaves. His ox flashed to his mind, and he immediately got to his feet, looking. But he soon thought that it was more likely that a wild boar had been there.

He walked and walked around the mountainside, down into the valley and up again, but could catch no glimpse of his animal. He dragged his feet upward along the stream that flowed crookedly down from the mountain. Tired and disheartened, he began to make his way by setting one foot ahead, clasping his hands on his knee, and pulling the other leg up.

As he came in sight of a lantern at a tile-roofed gate, he walked faster to reach the huge temple. The curved roof made a silhouette against the sickle-moon sky. A pagoda cast a long shadow on the grass like a boat with high masts anchored in the night. Soon he was looking across an open yard, enclosed only by flowerbeds, to the doors of the temple. Behind the lighted paper doors of the prayer rooms moved the shadows of monks, who in slow tones chanted, *"Ma soo ri . . . Soo soo ri . . . Sa ba ha!"* With the chanting came the tapping of a hollow wooden clapper.

An erect, elderly figure emerged from the darkness into the lighted part of the yard and began to stroll back and forth between shadow and light. Chun Bok thought the gray-clad figure in straw shoes must be an ancient senior monk who never strayed from the path to Buddha. Chun Bok moved quietly as he entered the gateway.

A gentle voice exclaimed, "Child, where did you come from?" The monk came with slow steps to Chun Bok.

"I left Butterfly Valley to find my ox and lost my way," Chun Bok could only mutter in a faint voice, clearing his throat.

The monk said in welcome, "As long as you are in Buddha's place you have not lost your way. You will lose nothing if you see the world with your inner eyes." The monk's cheeks below his close-cropped hair were pale with the glow from the lamplight. "Child, you will sleep with one of the young followers tonight." Pointing to a spot behind the living quarters, he kindly instructed, "Take a morning bath in the rivulet and join us for breakfast. Tomorrow's sun will help you find your way and your ox."

Touched with reverence for the monk's age and saintliness, Chun Bok obeyed, following him toward a house in the side yard. There were sounds in the thatch-roofed wing, where a soft light was burning.

❀ *12* ❀

CHUN BOK was awakened the next morning by the solemn clang of the temple gong.

"Why is it," he thought sleepily, "that it seems to be sounding for me? Hundreds of years this gong has sounded from the temple through all the countryside, and yet I feel as if it rang just for me."

Each clang faded away as if chased by the next, and in the intervals came the chanting of prayers. Chun Bok stirred in bewilderment, trying to recall how he had gotten to wherever he was.

Someone had been with him when he went to sleep. Still under his quilt, he turned and found only the neatly folded quilt of the young monk who had plagued him with conversation while he was dropping off to sleep. The novice had told him to go to Pestle to see the ox match and ask around the holiday crowd about his animal. Then the ox contest had led to the young monk's eager whispered talk about the junior monks' football team, the victories it had won, and how it could have defeated even the middle school team in Pusan if the senior monks had allowed the players to eat meat once in a while, instead of the eternal pumpkin stew.

Chun Bok remembered that, flat on his back, the boy had kicked his leg high in the air by way of illustration, reminding Chun Bok unhappily of his attempt to kick a ball with a straw shoe that flew higher than the ball.

Chun Bok opened the sliding door and came out of the room. The eastern sky was growing red. He breathed deep of the crisp morning air as he put on his straw shoes and walked on the dewy earth. Water was dripping like a string of pearls from a bamboo pipe into a wooden trough where a gourd dipper floated among the lotus.

By following the pipe, Chun Bok found a way through the wall of trees, though he had to walk sidewise to pass. The waters of a fast-flowing stream glittered ahead of him, and he ran toward it, undressing as he went. He stood on a flat stone and let the cold, clean water run around and over his feet. He scooped it up in his hands and poured it on his shoulders. Joy welled up in him like a full spring from a mysterious source. His muscles bounded. He clenched his fists and shouted loudly, "Aha! Aha!"

His cry came back to him in echo. He raised his head toward the narrow strips of sky above him, between the lofty trees. He fixed his eyes at the two patches of the blue until he forgot what he was looking at. Then they grew familiar — the water color of eyes. He realized he was thinking of his mother, her stern yet gentle gaze. The two marks of blue looked lovely. For an instant, she seemed to watch him bathe. It had been a long time since his mother had helped him bathe. She would make a cup of her two palms and pour water on his grateful body. Bending over to swish his hands in the water, he wondered when and why he had begun to feel ashamed of the water-blue eyes which were his. Was she still asleep? Or was she keeping her eyes on the gate, waiting?

Realizing that he was staying away too long, Chun Bok hurried back to the temple.

In the yard, birds sang from the jujube tree, the

music from their yellow beaks seeming to take turns with the soft tinkling of the pagoda's windbell. Down the white steppingstones came the senior monk in a brownish yellow silk robe, carrying his prayer bell and stick. Behind him a young monk in a blue robe carried a tray on which was a brass bowl of steaming rice. The smell of burning incense came to Chun Bok's nostrils and he knew the monks were offering food and prayers to Buddha.

The younger one said with calm dignity, "I was looking for you. You have heard people say, 'Morning meal as early as at the temple'!"

Chun Bok recognized the voice as that of the very boy who last night had talked of football and of eating fish and meat instead of eternal pumpkin stew. How could he have changed so much overnight?

In the dining room, a bronze statue of Buddha stood in a central niche flanked by paintings of his disciples. Torn between shyness and curiosity, Chun Bok glanced often at these ancient pictures as he sat at breakfast with six junior monks, the youngest less than his age.

The meal was rice and barley mixed with sorghum, seaweed browned in corn oil, soya sauce, bean sprouts, and the "eternal" pumpkin stew.

Afterwards, he alone made his way across the yard to the thatched wing to clean the room in which he had slept. It was so quiet that the dripping of water from a bamboo pipe into a pool sounded large. Under the roof of the quarters a big barrel-shaped copper gong with its padded sticks hung from a horizontal pole. Disregarding it in its silence, birds flew to and from a hanging nest at a corner pillar. Their odd shiny eyes brought back his unhappy thought. Trying not to remember "Bird Eye," he swept the oil-paper-covered floor with unnecessary vigor and vim. As he picked up and dusted a hand mirror propped in the corner of the room, he saw his reflection. He peered hard at it; his gaze settled on the blue eyes. For a moment the blue eyes seemed to be all there was of the little face. He spoke to the reflection: "You, fish eye, bird eye, I hate you! How can two small marks of blue be so important?"

As though they were hurt, water gathered in the corners of the eyes and glistened, reflecting the brightness of the morning sun. Wondering what the monk had meant by "inner eyes," he sought to touch the reflection. His hand reached behind the mirror, but there was nothing, yet there must be something. The two blue eyes he could see but couldn't touch became hazy and blurred into those of his mother, and somewhere within, Omanee seemed to be weeping. Tears poured out from under her eyelids, as he had seen them do when he refused to go to school. Chun Bok dropped the mirror and cried, "Oma!"

It was strange that what he missed most was his mother's eyes; no matter where he went they seemed to watch him. Didn't the two patches of early sky seem to him like Omanee's blue gaze? And why did her eyes, rather than anything else, come to his mind first? Was this his inner eye?

❀ *13* ❀

CHUN BOK bid farewell to the senior monk returning from his morning walk. The monk took off his wide-brimmed hat and blessed Chun Bok with the words, "May your inner eyes guide your way to hear and see yourself." The young novice came out of the gateway and walked with Chun Bok on the sunken path with its row of red balsam flowers. He showed him a forked road that would eventually lead to the ox fight place. Down to the narrow strip of the valley, pines, hickories, firs and alders shaded the thin grass lane. In a green ricefield below, a cow was grazing in the shadow of a broad alder. He moved his steps fast, thinking of his own ox.

When he reached the big road in the valley, Chun Bok saw several farmers leading their oxen, one of which carried a blanket bundle on his back. By following the farmers, Chun Bok learned that they came from across three or four mountains to join the ox match.

Chun Bok met more people at each bend of the mountain road. In family groups, children in their new, many-colored clothes, their cheeks daubed with pink powder, trotted ahead of their elders.

At the mountain pass, Chun Bok could see the white crowds in the valley below, where several canopies blew in the wind. The people formed a big circle on the smooth gray ground. Outside the circle, shiny-coated oxen were dotted here and there amid the people; they bellowed and stamped their forefeet restlessly. Some farmers carried banners and drums, horns and other noisemakers, and wore on their heads paper hats in shapes of roses, camellias and dragons. Going down the grassy slope of the mountain, Chun Bok saw a group of women singing and dancing. A woman was beating a kettle and singing:

Lark, lark in the Fifth Moon,
A butterfly hunts a flower . . .

A group of boys went by singing:

> *Look at me, look at me*
> *As if you had found a flower*
> *In the Twelfth Moon.*

One of the women chuckled at the song: "Oh you bunch of green peppers puffed up by the spring wind!"

Still farther down, another group of young women and girls gathered around a crooked pine. A swing was tied on a limb of the tree and the small girls swung high and gracefully. There were a few girls from the Butterfly Valley school. A few big boys stood a little apart from the girls, commenting on each swinger and giggling: "A pumpkin, too fat." "Formosa potato, too heavy." "Jerky as a scared hen."

Chun Bok was surprised to see Jung Lan appear in the circle to take her turn on the swing. In her holiday clothes, she clutched the rope and pushed her feet firmly against the swing board. She swung even higher, her long blue skirt swelling and the cords of her orange bodice floating into the air. She swung almost as high as the branch to which the swing was tied, and came back swift as a swallow.

There was loud applause when the graceful swinger slid off the board.

He wished he could go to talk with Jung Lan and her friends. Feeling as if his feet were holding him back, Chun Bok walked down the valley to look for his ox.

❀ *14* ❀

CHUN BOK searched all through the milling crowd but was unable to find his animal. Finally he went to the large circle that had formed to watch the ox fights. As one ox limped away hurriedly from the circle, the spectators roared, beat their drums and pans, some whirling about in a triumphant dance. A judge in the arena threw an orange scarf over a nut-brown ox and led the victor to a large canopy under which sat several men, each with a yellow band around his arm. Not far from the canopy stood the boys from Butterfly Valley, their faces in the direct morning sun as clear as the dazzle of an abalone. Pal Min frowned, yet his mouth managed a laugh.

Chun Bok wondered whether they were laughing at him. His anger boiled bitterly. "I will straighten their big noses and bring their chins down. I will not run away from those school fellows but beat them, every one of them," he said to himself, holding his fist tight.

Two owners brought forth their animals. Once Chun Bok found them not his, his eyes turned back toward the schoolboys. When they moved inside the arena, a ruddy-faced judge scared them into retreat with a threatening, swinging arm.

Near the canopy, Chun Bok saw the cattle-shoe man squatting foremost in the line of people. He was wearing clean white trousers tied at the ankle with red ribbons.

In the arena the two heavy heads of the oxen clashed. Now one, now the other ox freed himself from the other's onslaught, then one tried to find a way out of the circle, the other ox chasing.

After the crowd's laughing, shouting and beating of drums had subsided, the next two brown animals entered. As the oxen were brought to face each other, each owner took the halter off his animal. But the animals, instead of fighting, walked away with heads down.

The farmers with hats of paper flowers came out, blowing horns, banging drums. While music and dancing went on, a megaphone immediately announced another fight; the owners' names and their villages.

A cocksure fellow led his rugged animal all around the inside of the circle. His hand felt over his ox's fine lines and the set of his head on those heavy shoulders as if pointing them out to the crowd. He smiled and waved to win the sympathy of the spectators. A farmer beside Chun Bok shouted proudly, "It came from our Hempfield!" The man scowled when the entrance of the other ox was cheered with all the noisemakers. The crowd exclaimed when they heard that the ox had come all the way from Pusan. The animal shook his body and pawed the earth as he was led by a round fat man.

The approaching ox looked familiar. Chun Bok stepped forward to watch the animal closely. His heart began to beat loudly. The ox was the same dark yellow as his — yes, heavier through his middle than most oxen, with good balance as he placed his heavy legs at an outward slant. He saw his ox's same wide nostrils and long sharp horns. He walked toward his ox.

"Take that urchin off the grounds!" From behind Chun Bok rose shrill impatient voices.

Chun Bok felt strange hands dragging him off. "That ox is mine!" Chun Bok cried, pointing at the ox. He struggled to be free of the man, kicking, and trying to bite the arms that carried him away. He cried, "The one with those long curved horns is mine! It is not from Pusan!" But he was thrown from the circle of spectators and landed on his seat with a bang. Someone grabbed him by his cloth belt. Chun Bok could not pull loose. He hit the ground with his fist, crying and watching his ox.

The round, fat man had already yanked the halter off Chun Bok's animal. In hasty response, the Hempfield man released his ox. The two fighters did not plunge into butting. They measured each other with glaring eyes. As the Hempfield ox swirled toward his opponent's flank, Chun Bok's ox turned his square head skillfully. There came the strong clash of horns. Chun Bok closed his eyes. The spectators rose and shouted. Both oxen lowered their heads to the ground, pushed against each other with great force, then separated, eyed each other, advanced again, and twisted their clashing horns together.

They shifted ground first to one side, then to the other.

The man behind Chun Bok was no longer gripping his cloth belt. Chun Bok sprang up and ran to stop the fight. The round, fat man was walking up and down, clapping his hands and encouraging Chun Bok's ox. Men shouted, "That urchin again! Haul him out quickly!"

A judge with a yellow band turned to Chun Bok to catch him. Chun Bok quickly darted around the oxen. He tried to plead with his ox to run away with him, but the fight became faster and fiercer. He ran close to his ox each time someone tried to grab him. Chun Bok's ox often stepped out and let the other spend his charge on nothing, then followed him with a thrust to the flanks. For a brief moment, the two oxen separated. The opposing ox dripped saliva; from the corners of his enlarged eyes he looked for an escape.

Chun Bok's ox made the next move. The Hempfield ox lowered his horns to stop the butting. The two pairs of horns met, grinding. Trying to free his horns, the Hempfield ox backed quickly, turning his head. Chun Bok's ox followed his moves and threw all the force of his wide head and shoulders into his opponent. The Hempfield ox stumbled but jumped up limping. As Chun Bok's ox moved to aim at his opponent's belly, the Hempfield ox turned and ran. The crowd lost no time making way for the fleeing animal. Chun Bok, open-mouthed, stood still.

His ox ran after the Hempfield animal, but many men headed off the chasing ox. The merrymakers danced and whirled to the drums and kettles.

❀ *15* ❀

THE round, fat man slipped the bamboo ring through the nose of Chun Bok's ox and pulled him by the ring to the canopy. Chun Bok hurried after his ox, speaking up loud: "It is my ox!" He pointed to the fat man, who seemed shorter than his ox. "The man is not the owner."

His animal, jumpy, breathed heavily as the judges under the canopy rose.

Chun Bok grabbed a ruddy-faced judge by his sleeve, pleading, "I lost this ox yesterday. He is my ox!"

"Who is this mad boy?" The judge shook Chun Bok off his arm.

"Is this fellow — this small green pepper — out of his mind?" the fat man shouted.

Chun Bok insisted, "He is mine! My mother and I brought him from Cheju Island."

"You — you little liar." The fat man's small eyes popped upward as he continued, "I'll stuff a big rag in your lying mouth." Then he raised his fat hand and slapped Chun Bok. Chun Bok cried louder, "The way the horns curve, the iron-shod hooves — he is mine. You are not his owner."

The ox slowly turned and lifted his square jaw toward Chun Bok. Biting his lower lip with his large front teeth, the fat man moved forward to grab Chun Bok. Boys ran in, yelling, "The winner came from our village!" They were the schoolchildren. They drew nearer, panting with haste and excitement. The fat man turned to the boys, but they kept shouting. Pal Min appealed to someone nearby. "Yes, that is his ox. His mother has been looking for him and his ox."

The ruddy-faced judge, thick veins forming in his neck, shouted, "You little devils! If you don't go away, I will beat all of you."

Chun Bok turned his eyes upon the gathering crowd. "This is my animal."

Someone under the canopy said, "Bring your father. We do not have time to talk with children."

"Ask the ox which one is the owner. He will answer," another joked. Many laughed. Even the fat man forced himself to laugh as if he were no longer taking the children seriously. His laughter sounded as hollow as a cracked earthen jar. Chun Bok's voice broke. His ox lowed at the narrowing circle.

The ruddy-faced judge lifted a whip to push back the onlookers in front of the canopy. "Out of the way!" he shouted. "With my eyes closed, I will whip anyone standing in my way." His whip, snapping, hit some boys. They rubbed their arms and shoulders but did not run away.

"Wait," a heavy voice demanded. "I have shod that ox." It was the cattle-shoe man jostling his way through the onlookers.

Under the canopy an old man in a satin gown rose and asked, "What is all this?"

The cattle-shoe man explained rapidly, "I thought it strange when the announcer said this animal came from Pusan City, and tried to recall where I had seen him, until I saw that boy."

The round, fat face turned pale. He stuttered several times before he could say, "He is a liar. I

am surrounded by small and big liars. You meet twenty customers every day and you can't remember every one."

"I didn't say I remember every one." The cattle-shoe man's stumpy finger came right above Chun Bok's nose. "When I saw his blue eyes, I recognized him."

"It is true," the boys put in. "He is the only one who has blue eyes. He is our friend. He is the real owner!"

The cattle-shoe man spoke slowly. "This blue-eyed boy brought me this animal."

"You liar, how dare you say this animal . . . ?" the round man shouted and rubbed his nose with the flat of his fat hand.

Without answering, the cattle-shoe man stooped over, his ears reddening. His hand passed over the ox's low-hung belly, then the knee joint of the ox as he raised its hoof. The newly fastened iron burned white in the sun. He breathed noisily, saying, "This is the brand-new iron shoe I fixed yesterday." The ox's head and dewlap stirred.

"Look! He is leaving!" a boy warned. Chun Bok saw the round, fat man slyly moving to skirt the crowd. He had not gone far when a judge called after him, "Stop the ox thief."

The thief was quickly surrounded by strong farmers. He cringed, whimpered, struggling to free himself.

Chun Bok held his ox by the bamboo ring and faced the men under the canopy. One commented, "This boy has strange eyes. They must be either very lucky or very unlucky." Chun Bok felt everyone looking into his eyes, but he could look at them gladly.

The old man in his graceful gown said to Chun Bok, "Now that you won one match, you will fight in the fifth match, and fight again if you win."

Chun Bok bowed to leave, looking at the old man. The men under the canopy clapped.

The boys walked on both sides of Chun Bok and his ox. "The Butterfly Valley ox won the match!" they shouted triumphantly. "It's our ox."

Chun Bok took his ox into the cool shade of a pine to rest him. As the boys' hands caressed the ox's huge glossy flank, a strange child whispered in Pal Min's ear. Pal Min answered loudly, "Yes, you may touch our ox once."

A plump boy brought a rope halter to Chun Bok and volunteered, "I will go and tell the girls at the swinging."

Another said, "Our ox must have much to eat to win many fights." They all left hurriedly to gather grasses.

Shouts and clamors rose from the arena. Chun Bok could hardly believe that his gentle ox had fought a rough ox and won. As Chun Bok's hand touched his temple to pet him, the ox jerked his head. There was a reddish bruise between his horns. Fright chilled Chun Bok. Another fight would worsen the wound and hurt his animal. Chun Bok shook as violently as if it were he himself who would have to fight again. He did not want his ox to fight.

He saw the girls hurrying toward him. Chun Bok quickly tied the rope halter to the bamboo ring and pulled it to move away. The chunky boy who had gone to get the girls called, "Chun Bok." He did not turn to answer. He pressed forward in the crowd to reach the road, shouting for the right of way for his animal. He heard Jung Lan calling him, "Chun Bok, where are you going?" but he kept on.

❀ *16* ❀

WHEN Chun Bok reached the slope of a hill, he stopped to catch his breath. A call came from below the mountain: "Chun Bok! Chun Bok!" From the height he could discern Butterfly Valley boys and girls rushing up the winding path. Chun Bok was once again on his feet running with his ox.

The boys, calling "Chun Bok! Chun Bok!," ran after him. They came closer. They would take his ox for the fight.

After reaching the other side of the hill, he felt the boys had stopped chasing him. Panting, he clutched his ox's shoulder and laid his head on the animal's strong neck. The ox's ear, cool and silky, touched his warm cheek. He whispered, "You were a

good fighter when you had to fight, but I won't let anyone make you fight again." Breezes from the pass were cool on his chest and lifted his spirit. His ox stirred and he raised his head. Three boys darted out from behind the mountain bend. Pal Min, his hands around his mouth, trumpeted, "Chun Bok. Your mother and teacher want you to come home."

Swiftly he moved off the road, making his way through wild thorny bush, and came out before a small river. He took off his shoes and rolled his trousers high. Then he rushed into the stream, tugging his ox hard by the halter. The ox raised his head over the water that reached to his knee joints, then to his belly. The pursuers in their holiday clothes would not dare to wade the muddy creek. Chun Bok, his eyes on the boys beyond the thorny bush, drove his ox up on the opposite bank and began to wipe the mud off his feet on the grass. A sudden sharp pain in his right foot jolted him and sent him to his knees. A wild bee's sting, he thought. He bent to see the wounded spot and immediately knew it was something worse. There were two small wounds.

A triangular head followed by an arm's length of red-spotted green zigzagged away.

"Poison snake!" cried Chun Bok, clasping his leg. "Poison snake bit me," he shouted loud.

Soon the three boys darted out on the other side of the creek. They splashed through the stream to Chun Bok. More boys followed, churning the water.

A lanky boy, arriving first, said, "Oh, it was probably not a poison snake. Are you sure?"

"Yes," groaned Chun Bok, "a real one!"

The lanky boy at once took off the long cloth belt he wore. While he held his trousers with his hand, his friends wound the belt tight around Chun Bok's shin.

As they moved around, the clay mud oozed out of their shoes. Their wet trousers stuck to their legs. Pal Min took his jackknife from his pocket and talked rapidly. Drops of sweat ran down Chun Bok's hot face.

The boys held Chun Bok's arms and legs while Pal Min cut across each fang mark and into the surrounding flesh. The blood flowed to the green grass. Chun Bok gritted his teeth, moaning.

Girls were coming, their faces ash-white. A few were wiping their eyes with their silk sleeves. A small girl swept an angry glance around the boys, who merely watched the operation. "Don't stand there doing nothing!" she demanded. "We should find the snake and kill him."

The boys began to search for the snake, each boasting, "I will kill him." Some lifted rocks that lay close together.

Jung Lan came with a poultice of pounded leaves and bound it on the wounded foot with handkerchieves. The boys lifted Chun Bok to the broad back of his ox and helped him to sit up. They held him from both sides so that he would not fall as they led the ox forward. The road ahead of him became blurred and dim. Chun Bok was too weak to cling to the ox. Finally, with the help of many outstretched arms, Chun Bok dismounted from his ox and lay on the grass, groaning. Several ran to a nearby house to borrow a rush-woven litter. He imagined his house with red peppers in the garden, then alone in darkness Omanee's eyes, only her eyes looking at him. Chun Bok moaned, "Oma, I shouldn't have left you, my Oma."

❀ *17* ❀

CHUN BOK did not realize it was his own porch until his mother rushed forward with a strangled cry, "My boy! Oh, what evil thing has happened to you?"

His mouth quivered as he tried to speak, but his tongue was too heavy. He placed his hand over his throat, parched and dry.

Omanee looked at his bandaged foot, then turned to the boys for explanation. Their chests rose and fell with heavy breathing. "Chun Bok was bitten by a poison snake," a tall boy panted. "We took turns carrying him in the litter."

Soon the rim of a white water bowl touched his lips. Chun Bok drank what tasted like the icy water from the well at the foot of a winding mountain path. "He shed much blood, Chun Bok's mother," Chun Bok heard someone saying. "Our teacher told us to give little water to a wounded soldier."

Omanee did not give him a second bowl of water. Chun Bok enviously watched the bearers gulping water from the jar. Omanee put an arm under Chun Bok's shoulder and clasped his hand to her breast. Her face twisted with her effort to hold back her tears.

The young carriers dusted off their trousers and helped Omanee lift Chun Bok into the room. The oil-papered floor was cool and pleasant, and Chun Bok raised his eyes toward the boys in thanks. Omanee furtively took some coins from her sewing box and followed the boys to the porch. She said modestly, "If it is not enough for candy, buy sweet potatoes." But the boys left without taking any money.

Chun Bok suddenly remembered his ox. Had they sent his animal back to the fight? When Omanee returned to the room, he cried repeatedly, "Where is my ox? Where is my ox?"

"He is in the shed. They brought the ox home at the same time you arrived, Bok," Omanee answered, and soothed his swollen leg with a cold cloth.

Chun Bok wished he could run into the shed to throw his arms around the animal's neck, and held Omanee's hand tight.

"The teacher told me what happened yesterday." Caressing his hot head, she went on, "You don't have to go to school."

Her sad gaze reminded him of the reflection he had seen in the hand mirror while he was in the temple. Two hot tears came to his eyes. More came. "Oma, I will never leave you again. I will work on a farm to pay back the school."

Tired and weak, Chun Bok soon closed his wet eyes and dropped off to sleep.

Several times in the night he woke and turned on his side to see Omanee near him. He listened to his animal stirring on his trampling feet.

With the first light of day came dawn noises in the neighborhood — someone thrashing barley, someone calling from barn to house; in his garden birds sang. Omanee brought in hot rice broth and fed it to him with pickled crab sauce. Chun Bok sat up halfway, leaning against his bed quilt, his haggard face toward the shed.

From the gateway came the sounds of forced coughings and footsteps. Chun Bok saw the herb man with his horsehair hat followed by the teacher. Omanee tried to rouse Chun Bok, saying, "The doctor and teacher kindly came last night when you were asleep." She smoothed her hair to invite the doctor into the room.

The old man told her, "No, no, please let Chun Bok sit still and go on feeding him. I know you won't need me, but I came along with the teacher." He sat crossed-legged on the porch and talked to her. "The crab sauce is good to counteract the venom."

As the teacher came near the porch, he took off his straw hat. The doctor started to speak with the teacher. "I praised your students for the quick way they treated the snake poison. They told me they learned it in school." The old man laughed good-naturedly and went on puffing his long bamboo pipe. "We old men used to think that these children go to school only to gang up, run and sing, and come home only to complain of their empty stomachs." His tall horsehair hat nodded as though agreeing with his words: "No — they must be learning some valuable lessons."

The teacher moistened his lips and, squeezing his hat, said in a low, earnest voice, "We are hoping Chun Bok will come back to school."

The old man laid a hand on his knee as he rose, saying, "We taught him proverbs and stories. He retains them well. He will learn well in school."

Omanee laid aside the breakfast tray and stepped out on the porch. She and the teacher respectfully followed the old man as he was leaving. He answered their worried looks: "Chun Bok is young and strong. Unlike an old man, he doesn't have to wait for another moon."

Before Omanee and the teacher returned to the porch, young voices and the shuffling of feet came from beyond the gateway. "Chun Bok's friends!" Omanee greeted. Chun Bok saw the quick line of boys and girls entering the yard, a few hurrying to the shed. The teacher told them, "Be quiet! You should have sent only your monitor! Be quiet!"

Chun Bok crawled out to the porch to meet the young visitors. The morning light made him squint. He felt dizzy. Jung Lan put a sprig of pear blossom before him. "Please accept our good wishes," she said.

Pal Min stepped forward, his hands reaching into his bulging pockets. He drew out an egg from each and presented the two eggs to Omanee.

"You children have been very kind to your new

friend." She seemed to force her voice. "When Chun Bok is well, he will go out with his ox to farm and earn money to pay back everything he owes."

"We would be glad to hire Chun Bok's ox for our school farm if he is willing to come to school."

Chun Bok saw his friends put their heads together in front of the teacher, while they talked eagerly. "Yes, after the next rain we will have to have a strong ox to plow the field for onions and turnips, won't we?" "He defeated the Hempfield ox. He is stronger than most oxen." "We should fix a room in the school barn for Chun Bok's ox."

The teacher urged his students, "All right, all right. Everybody leave." He came to Chun Bok and, patting his arm, said gently, "When you can walk, come to school."

Someone spoke up: "Chun Bok could come even tomorrow. He could ride his ox to school. I will help him mount and dismount from his ox."

The teacher turned to him, smiling. "That is a good, worthy thought." Then he asked, raising his own hand, "Who wants to take Chun Bok's ox for a good breakfast of the sun and grass?"

Many stretched out their hands, almost touching

the teacher's face. "I am the first who asked. I am the first."

The teacher's fingers held the stem of his glasses lest they fall off, while he grumbled, "Whoever said 'I am the first' won't get it."

They stretched their hands right before his glasses. "I am the last! I am the last!"

The square-faced animal was already being led out by several willing hands. As each tried to hold the halter, the teacher took the rope.

Chun Bok rose to be near his ox but was too weak to step down from the porch. He clung to the porch pillar. The ox opened his mouth and stretched his heavy neck, greeting him with a low moo. A girl standing by the teacher said, "If you haven't had time to prepare lunch this morning, I will give you mine." The teacher scratched his head in embarrassment and hastily started to leave.

Chun Bok watched his big tan animal leaving, surrounded by his friends. If he had had ordinary dark eyes, the cattle-shoe man might not have recognized him as the owner of that animal, he thought.

Boys kept shouting to one another to clear the way for the ox as they jostled along the narrow shore path.

Then the cries changed as the way led between the green rice paddies, then their singing floated back home.

> *Let's sing with crickets,*
> *Lets sing with green frogs,*
> *Till he returns.*

After the song had died in the distance, Chun Bok still tried to follow his ox in the procession. How far on the way would they be by now?

He imagined himself hurrying on his ox's back to catch up with them, then dismounting from his ox to enter the schoolroom. In his reverie, he saw those faces piling out over the windowsills to welcome him, and he smiled into their eyes.

Omanee carried the pear sprig in a bottle into the room, then put Pal Min's eggs into the basket hung in the breezeway under the eaves. Chun Bok tried to move, but his foot pained him. His wound might last long; he was impatient. As Omanee came to help him into the room, he asked her, "Before my foot gets better, may I go to school on my ox's back?"

She did not say anything, but a smile quivered on her lips. Watching her blue eyes wrinkling, moistening happily, he knew his were laughing, too. Were

those, he wondered, his inner eyes that had wept behind the mirror? "Oma." He held her arms. "While
I was away, I remembered your eyes most. Blue eyes
are lucky."